THE MAMMOTH ACADEMY

OSCAR WAS

A WOOLLY MAMMOTH.

AND SO WAS

ARABELLA.

SOME OF THE OTHER
PUPILS AT
THE
MAMMOTH
ACADEMY
FLY LIVED IN
THE ACADEMY BUT
WASN'T A PUPIL.
CAVE
CAT

ORMSBY

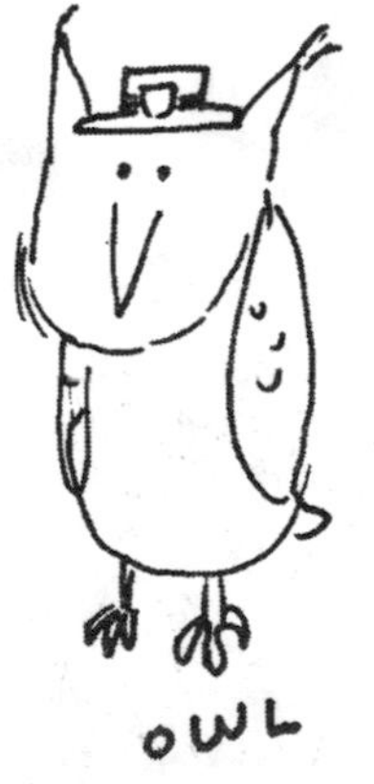

OWL

PRUNELLA

FOX

A FEW MORE PUPILS OF
THE
MAMMOTH
ACADEMY

ROGER

REGINALD
RHONDA
REMI
REX
RUFUS
REENIE

CAVE
BEAR
GIANT
GROUND
SLOTH

Some of the PUPILS OF The...

PROFESSOR UGH
Professor UGH teaches THE PUPILS of the CAVE SKOOL

THE REALLY REALLY HIGH MOUNQAINS
CAVE
CAVE SKOOL
THE CLIFFS
THE MARSHY MARSH
THE WILD LANDS
N
W
E
S
THE ICY PLAINS

THE MAMMOTH ACADEMY

THE ICE LAKE

THE HEROS →

THE ALMOST IMPOSSIBLE TO CROSS GLACIER

MAP OF THE MAMMOTH LANDS

For Anne McNeil

First published in Great Britain in 2007
by Hodder Children's Books

1

A Catalogue record for this book is available from the British Library

ISBN-13: 978 0 340 93030 4

Printed in the UK by CPI Bookmarque, Croydon, CR0 4TD

The paper and board used in this paperback by Hodder Children's Books
are natural recyclable products made from wood grown in sustainable forests.
The manufacturing processes conform to the environmental
regulations of the country of origin.

Hodder Children's Books
a division of Hachette Children's Books
338 Euston Road
London NW1 3BH

THE
MAMMOTH
ACADEMY
in TROUBLE!

CHAPTER 1
THE NEW TERM

Oscar was a Woolly Mammoth, and so was Arabella. They lived a long time ago in the Ice Age.

They had been having a terrific time on holiday, romping in snowfields, uncovering secret mountain paths, rooting out mountain berries and playing Ice Frisbee, but now it was time to go back to the Mammoth Academy for the new term.

THIS LETTER
ARRIVED BY MAMMOTH MAIL

Dear Student,

The new term is about to start tomorrow.

All First Years must bring with them:

1. A pair of safety goggles, safety gloves and a safety apron.

2. A pair of safety scissors.

3. A big pot of glue.

4. A big bottle of ink.

5. Fourteen lined exercise books ...

... and lots of brightly coloured material and other things to be used to prepare for the Founder's Fiesta.

The headmistress's speech will begin at 9am.
Lessons will follow straight away.

Signed

Professor Snout

Both Oscar and Arabella were looking forward to going back to the Academy, mainly because the new term would end in the fabulous Founder's Fiesta!

The Founder's Fiesta (along with Stinky Day *see note) is one of THE most exciting days in the Mammoth year. The whole Academy gets decorated with bunting and balloons. Cook bakes enormous Founder's Fiesta puddings. There are no lessons and no uniforms, but there is plenty of feasting and dancing until very late at night.

EVERYONE was excited about it!

NOTE:
Stinky Day is the one day of the year when all the pupils are allowed to get as smelly and messy as possible. Fox normally wins the contest.

On the first day back, as Oscar and Arabella walked across the icy wastes, the sun was shining and they were both in high spirits. They greeted the friendly Megaloceros as he helped them across the glacier.

Along the way lots of their school friends joined them and there was plenty of friendly banter.

'Hey, Fox, haven't seen you in ages! How are you doing?'

'I'm cool! How are you?'

'Look there's Giant Sloth and Prunella.' Prunella was Arabella's best friend at the Academy. She was also the smallest pupil in the whole school.

Arabella liked Prunella because she was fashionable and wore pretty bows. Prunella liked Arabella because she was clever and strong and would look after her in the busy school corridors.

'Hi there, Prunella!'

'Hi there, Arabella!'

Everyone was carrying big bundles of paper, books, ink and lots of things to be used to prepare for the Founder's Fiesta.

As more and more First Years joined the procession the level of excitement rose.

'Wooo!'

'Yeah!'

Until they arrived at the Mammoth Academy gates.

And suddenly everyone went very quiet . . .

WE IS GONNA GIT YOU!!!

WE IS GONNA GIT YOU!!

CHAPTER 2
NEW LESSONS

This wasn't the welcome back to the Academy that anyone had been expecting.

As the school assembled to hear the headmistress give her 'start the term' speech, you could have heard a pinecone drop.

'Welcome back, everyone.

'As you know, this term will end with the Founder's Fiesta. I hope you are all looking forward to it as much as I am.

'You will have noticed that some rather unpleasant graffiti has appeared outside the school gates. We think this could mean that there are humans about!

'In case you've forgotten, this is what they look like. They are wild and dangerous animals and are to be avoided! Take care when entering or leaving the school, stay close to your friends, and if anyone sees

anything suspicious contact a member of staff immediately.

'Here are your timetables. Off you go . . .'

HUMANS!
Humans are scary...
DID YOU HEAR...?
WHAT IS GOING TO HAPPEN?

After that they had lots of new lessons including science with Dr Van Der Graph.

'Right, everyone, put on your safety goggles, your safety aprons and your safety gloves.

'And now start mixing things in test tubes . . .'

Fox's test tube turned brown.

Oscar's test tube turned orange.

But Arabella's test tube started to fizz and spit tiny little silver sparks all over the place, finally going POOF! in a cloud of thick green smoke.

'Fascinating!' said Dr Van Der Graph. 'I think you have just made a scientific discovery!'

Next was dance class with Mrs Waft.

'This term we are going to learn a special dance to perform at the Founder's Fiesta.

'I want you all to imagine you are tiny feathers floating on the breeze . . .'

Last came art class with Professor Sable.

'Hi! This term we're going to make something AMAZING and INCREDIBLE with all the materials you have collected in the holidays, but first I want you to sketch out your ideas. You can do this on your own or in a group.

'Let's go!'

PRUNELLA'S IDEAS

Get pretty for the founders feast with...

Prunella's Beauty Parlour!!

GIANT SLOTH FELL ASLEEP...

ARABELLA'S SKETCHES
(SHE FILLED LOTS OF SHEETS

The Mammoth Mammoth Idea!

TRUNK

A HUGE mammoth sculpture
FRAMEWORK UNDERNEATH
OSCAR DIDN'T GET ON VERY WELL...
OSCAR WOZ ERE
HI-TECK

And then, BONG! BONG! BONG! The gong rang to tell everyone it was time to go home.

After their exciting day Oscar, Arabella and their friends had almost forgotten about the humans, but as they walked through the Academy gates to head home to the herds, they were quickly reminded that they must take extra care.

All the friends stayed very close together as they walked and nobody said much. Everybody was looking out for signs of trouble.

As they passed by the big forest Prunella thought she heard a strange noise.

'What's that?'

But her voice was so quiet that nobody heard her.

And she didn't want to alarm anyone unnecessarily, so she didn't mention it again.

CHAPTER 3
TROUBLE BREWING

The next day more graffiti had appeared outside the Academy walls.

Everyone agreed that this could only be the work of the Cave Skool humans.

'Look at the handwriting and the bad spelling,' said Arabella. 'It just *has* to be them.'

CAVE SKOOL ROOLS O.K.

Humans rock!

A window had also been smashed and an attempt made to break into Cook's kitchen. Cook was not pleased.

'If I ever get hold of the little savages I'll show 'em what for!'

The news spread round the Academy fast.

That day another art lesson was spent working on the Founder's Fiesta projects.

Prunella constructed Prunella's Beauty Parlour but with everyone so busy talking about the humans nobody went to visit.

Arabella began working on the Mammoth Mammoth. Oscar's project wasn't going too well so he asked if he could help. Arabella had just the job for him.

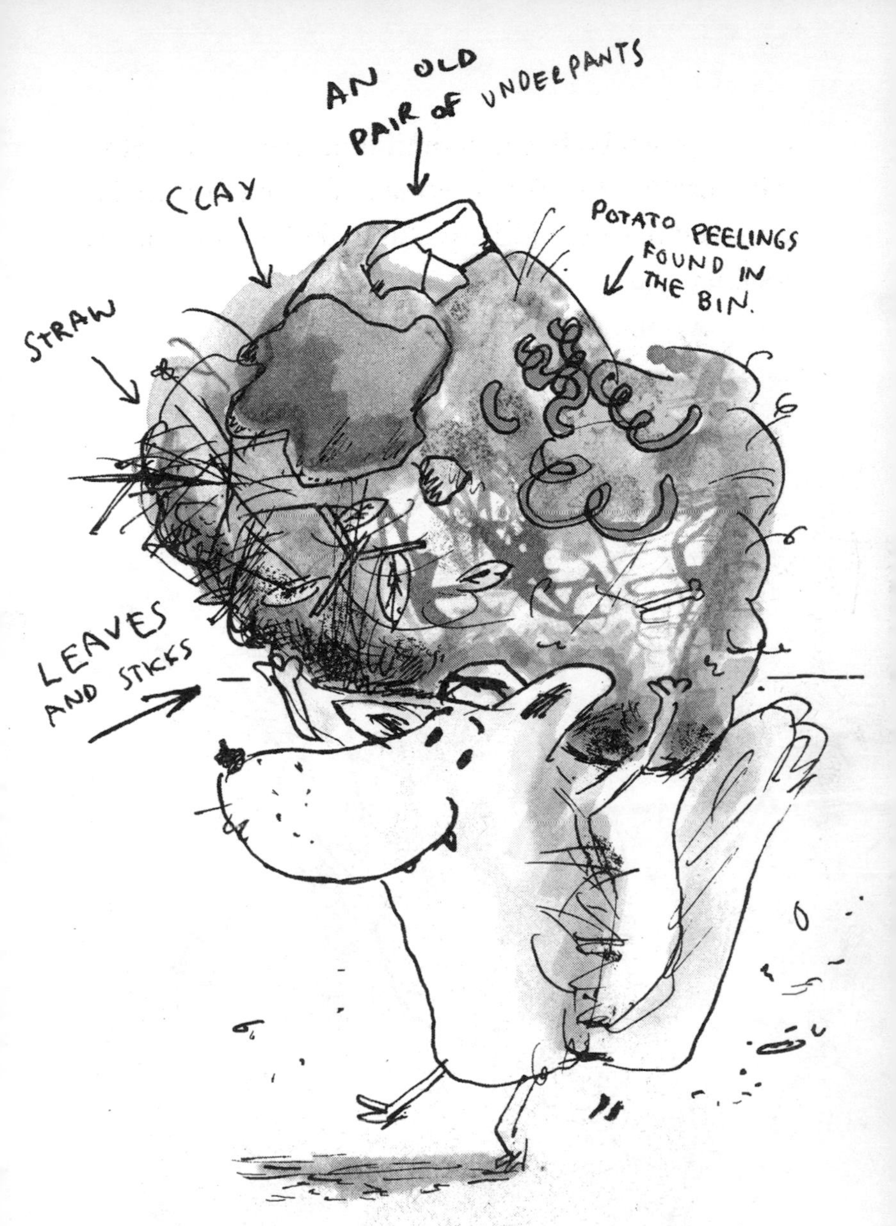

Fox thought it was looking a bit 'saggy' so he went off to find lots of things to stuff it with.

The rabbits suggested that wheels and a rope might make it easy to parade about. And Prunella, after the unsuccessful launch of the Beauty Parlour, wondered if she could join in and pointed out that a few bows might make it look prettier. Owl and Giant Sloth were keen to help too – in fact by the end of the lesson EVERYONE was involved in one way or another.

'This is going to be so cool when it's finished!'

'Yeah!'

Everyone agreed the class project was coming along very well indeed.

And suddenly, BONG! BONG! BONG! It was time for everyone to go home again.

WE is Gonna GIT YOU!!
CAVE SKOOL ROOLS O.K.
Humans rock!

As the friends passed through the graffiti-covered gates out on to the icy plains they noticed more signs of human activity.

The snow was littered with footprints, bits of rubbish and the odd bit of dung.

'Urgh! How disgusting!' exclaimed Prunella.

And then, as they passed by the forest, they could definitely hear strange noises in the trees that seemed to go something like,

'Nah-nah, nah-nah!'

'Ugh!'

Oscar, Arabella, Prunella, Fox and all their friends hurried homewards as fast as their legs would carry them.

CHAPTER 4
GIANT SLOTH

As the term carried on it quickly became apparent that Cave Skool humans definitely HAD moved into the area. There was more litter, dung and noise, and a huge stone flag went up in the forest that read 'CaVE SkOOL'.

There was also more graffiti.

What should have been the BEST term of the year was now rapidly turning out to be the WORST.

Every day as the mammoths and their friends went to and from the Academy the Cave Skool pupils would lurk in the woods, jeering and throwing snowballs.

The problem had got so bad that the friendly Megaloceros would have to accompany the pupils all the way from the glacier right up to the school gates.

One day, when Oscar, Arabella, Prunella and Giant Sloth went to go home after a busy day they found their path blocked. Ahead on the icy plains stood a group of twelve or thirteen humans, obviously pupils of Cave Skool.

'Ugh!' they said.

'I don't like the look of this,' said Arabella.

'What shall we do?' squeaked Prunella.

'Heh heh UGH!' sniggered the humans.

And suddenly, THWACK! Something landed near Arabella's foot, and FEEEEEEEE! Something whizzed towards Oscar, who just managed to hold up his school bag to deflect it.

'Ouch!' he said. 'That wasn't a snowball, that was an ICE BALL!'

'Quick! Run for it!'

But before they could run anywhere – THWACK!

A third much larger iceball hit Giant Sloth squarely in the face.

'HOOOOOOOOWWWWHHHLLLLLL!!!'

Giant Sloth let out the most deafening howl and gradually began to rise up on his back legs, waving his arms about. His eyes, normally halfshut, became wide like saucers and all his fur began to stand on end. He was obviously very VERY ANGRY!

'WHOOOOOOOOOOOOOOOAAAAAAA GGGGGRRRRRRRRRR!'

The Cave Skool humans dropped their half-finished iceballs, turned tail, and ran scrambling and howling back up the mountain into the woods.

CHAPTER 5
THE SPARKLEBANG CODE

News of Giant Sloth's heroism went round the school fast.

Everyone would wave and cheer as he passed in the corridors and teachers would let him sit quietly at the back of the class and rest.

Everyone hoped this might be the end of Cave Skool and that they would move miles away from the Academy and stop hanging around, making a nuisance of themselves.

With the humans out of the way for the time being life at the Academy began to go much better.

The caretaker managed to clear up the litter, scrub away the graffiti outside the gates and mend the broken window. All the students could walk to and from the Academy without worry and everyone could carry on preparing for the fast-approaching Founder's Fiesta.

Arabella, under the guidance of Dr Van Der Graph had made hundreds more discoveries.

TWINKLE
FIZZZ
WHEEEEEEEE!!

BANG!

After this, Dr Van Der Graph wrote up a code of use for all sparklebang mixtures.

THE SPARKLEBANG CODE

All sparklebang mixtures must be kept in a sealed box or tin.

All sparklebang mixtures must be kept away from hot things.

Always wear safety clothing.

Sparklebang mixtures can be dangerous and must only be used with the supervision of a responsible adult.

Signed

Dr Van der Graph

Then Fox had another one of his great ideas.

'Hey! Why don't we add some sparklebang mixtures to the Mammoth Mammoth? We could parade it about at the fiesta and then at the end of the evening start it sparkling. It would look amazing spitting and fizzing at night!'

Everyone agreed this was a splendid idea and so Dr Van Der Graph began joining in the art lessons, making special mixtures with Arabella and placing them carefully inside the Mammoth Mammoth.

Mrs Waft had also taken to spending her time in the art room as she said it would give her inspiration for the special Founder's Fiesta dance she was creating.

In fact everything was going really well until the storm arrived.

It started with a grey sky and a few wispy flakes of snow but by lunchtime the weather had got much worse.

The sky went black and the snow began falling so heavily that it was impossible for the mammoths to see their trunks in front of their faces. Students crossing the courtyards would have to shuffle along carefully in long lines holding each

other tail-to-trunk. The sharp wind cutting up from the icy plains caused huge snowdrifts to pile up against the walls and windows of the Academy.

By late afternoon the storm was at its height. None of the mammoth teachers could remember weather this bad, and some of them had very long memories indeed.

It was decided that it would be unwise to send the students home in such terrible weather so it was agreed that everyone would have to spend the night in the Academy instead.

The gates of the Academy were drawn closed and lots of blankets and sheets were brought down to the gymnasium so that it could act as a temporary sleeping area for students and staff. Ormsby said that the gym mats smelt of cheesy feet and that he wasn't keen to sleep on them but nobody listened to his complaints.

Cook shared out some hot soup and everyone tried to bed down and get some sleep, while outside the storm carried on raging.

For the first few days staying overnight in the Academy was quite fun, rather like a camping trip, or a sleepover at a friend's burrow. But everyone was relieved when after several days and nights the wind began to drop.

Most of the lower windows were completely covered with snow and ice, but from the higher windows the animals could peer out and survey the weather. At first nothing could be seen but some of the students reported seeing dark shapes moving outside and hearing strange noises.

'There are lots of animals out there!' exclaimed Fox.

'I think they are HUMANS!' shouted Oscar.

CHAPTER 6
SURROUNDED!

'It seems that we are surrounded,' said the headmistress. 'The humans have come back hungry and desperate for food and they want to eat US! All students will have to remain here until help arrives. Once the weather clears it shouldn't be too long.'

Lessons sort of carried on as normal with all the staff and pupils having to rush on to the roof every now and then to throw a few hundred snowballs to keep the humans at bay.

Outside, Cave Skool lessons seemed to be continuing as well.

TODAYS MENU
CABBAGE PORRIDGE
+
WHEAT HUSK CRACKERS

But it kept snowing.

And the Cave Skool humans didn't go away.

More days passed with Oscar, Arabella and their friends missing the herds and getting more and more anxious.

And then, with Cook unable to go shopping, food started to run out.

All that was left were wheat-husk crackers and cabbage. And though Cook did her best to be creative with her recipes they were not the most appetizing of foods to eat for breakfast, lunch AND dinner.

Toilet paper was getting low too. Professor Snout allowed each pupil three sheets a day, which, when you are the size of a woolly mammoth eating nothing but wheat-husk crackers and cabbage, is not very much at all.

More days passed and then the tusk paste ran out so everybody had cabbagy breath.

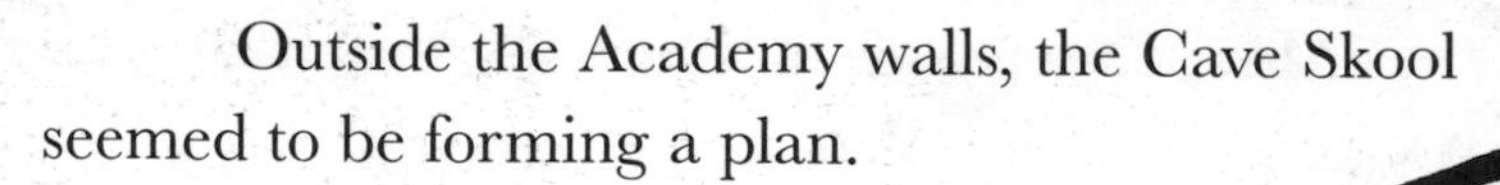

Outside the Academy walls, the Cave Skool seemed to be forming a plan.

THE PLAN

EVERYONE SHOUTS UGH!

UGH!

THEN EVERYONE ATTACKS AND TRIES TO GET IN.

THEN
FinD FOOD
Kill Food
COOK FOOD
EAT Food
FULL
tums
YUm!

Inside the Academy, the animals began to feel more worried and more scared.

And then the scratching started. Nobody was sure who got it first but the one thing that was certain was the cause of the problem – FLEAS!

The entire Academy was riddled with them!

Everyone was in a very dishevelled and miserable state. Even Fox, who normally enjoyed getting stinky, hung his head in dismay and looked at the floor.

'We're doomed! Doomed, I say!' moaned one mammoth.

'It's the end! The end of the Mammoth Academy and the end of us!' whined another.

'There's no hope,' mumbled a third.

'HEY!'

Everyone looked around to see who was speaking.

It was Prunella. She had climbed right up to the top of the Mammoth Mammoth and she was shouting at the top of her voice through a rolled-up piece of paper.

'HEY!' she shouted. 'That just simply isn't good enough!

'I may be the smallest animal in the Academy but there is no way that I am giving up!

'Have you all forgotten that it is the Founder's Fiesta TONIGHT? Well, I am not going to have it ruined by some silly humans!

'We can do anything if we pull together.

'We can beat the humans.

'We can beat the hunger.

'And we can beat the fleas!

'Anyone who comes to my beauty parlour will get their fleas combed out and a free new fur-style as well!'

CHAPTER 7
TEAMWORK

The queue for Prunella's Beauty Parlour went twice around the great hall but somehow Prunella managed to keep up with demand.

Briskly brushing, quickly combing and clipping, animal after animal was de-flead and given a snappy new style.

All the grooming was generating huge amounts of fluff and Arabella found just the use for it.

'It lends the Mammoth Mammoth such a realistic air, don't you think?'

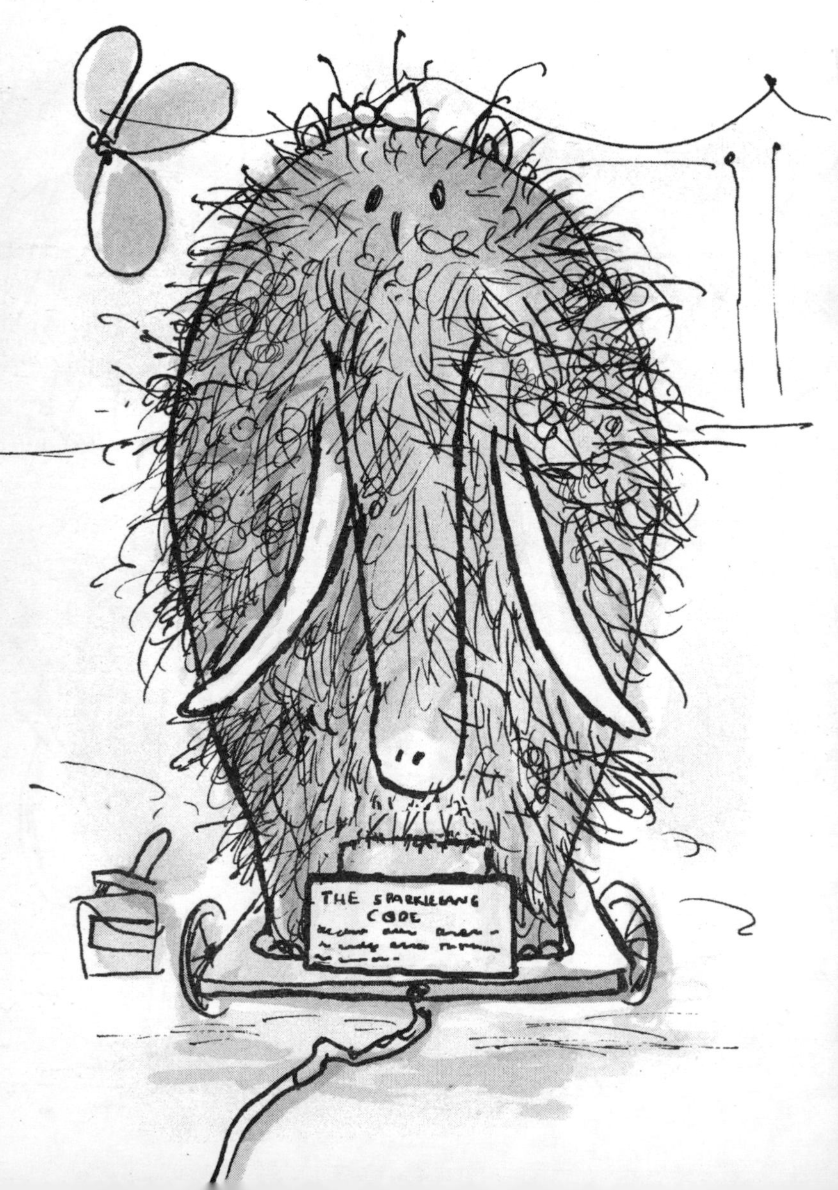

Finally, with everyone working together; the bunting was hung, the tables were laid, and the amazing and incredible Mammoth Mammoth was ready for the Founder's Fiesta Parade!

But suddenly, BONG!BONG!BONG!BONG!
BONG!

The special Alarm gong was sounded.

'THE HUMANS HAVE ENTERED THE ACADEMY! Quick! Everyone to the emergency escape tunnel!'

CHAPTER 8
THE MAMMOTH MAMMOTH

The unthinkable had happened. The humans had got into the Academy!

Hurriedly, the teachers ushered all the pupils down corridors, across courtyards and into the secret emergency escape tunnel. It was very dusty and very dark, but there was no other choice. The mammoths stumbled along blindly, following its twists and turns, climbing stair after stair, until they eventually emerged halfway up the mountain on to a small plateau.

THE ESCAPE TUNNEL

The small plateau

Meanwhile, inside the Academy, the humans were going berserk, jumping on tables, throwing bits of paper about and knocking over bookshelves.

'UGH UGH UGH!'

'UGH UGH UGH!'

They turned Cook's kitchen upside down, scattering jars, smashing plates, splintering cupboards and eating vast quantities of wheat-husk crackers and cabbage.

UGH!

UGH!

And then they found the Mammoth Mammoth.

For a few seconds they stood with their mouths wide open.

They had never seen anything like it. It was the BIGGEST mammoth they had ever seen – or, as they thought, the biggest DINNER they had ever seen.

‘FOOOOOOOOOD!’

‘YUUUMMM!’

Forming a circle around it, they began shouting ‘Ugh!’ and waving their spears and clubs.

The Mammoth Mammoth stared calmly back at them.

Then they began waving their spears and clubs more vigorously and shouting 'Ugh!' a bit louder.

The Mammoth Mammoth continued to stare calmly back at them.

UGH!
THE SPARKLEBANG CODE

With their confidence growing, one of them threw a spear at it. It missed so another human threw a spear at it. THOCK! This one landed quivering in its side. More spears followed, and ice balls and rocks and books and anything else that came to hand. After receiving several more direct hits a bit of the Mammoth Mammoth's ear came off and its head began to slump to one side.

A great cheer went up from the humans. It was defeated! FOOD!

THE SPARKLEBANG CODE

Professor Ugh advanced towards it. He grabbed the Sparklebang Code stuck carefully to the front of its trolley and ripped it off and put it in his mouth. It obviously didn't taste very nice because he spat it out again. 'Urrgghhhhh!'

Then he took a bite out of its leg. This seemed to taste better.

After realizing it was too big to push on his own he ordered the smaller humans to help him by pulling the two ropes handily attached to its front. They began wheeling it out of the great hall, through the gates, and towards their makeshift camp outside the Academy walls.

They couldn't wait to start feasting upon it.

'Ugh! Ugh! Ugh!'

'UGH! UGH! UGH!'

Huddled on top of the mountain, the mammoths looked on with interest.

CHAPTER 9
AT LAST!

As darkness fell, a hush descended on the mammoths and everyone settled down to watch what happened next. Some mammoths even climbed trees for a better view.

The humans wheeled the Mammoth Mammoth up to their campfire and began to stoke the fire up even higher.

Then they began to pluck and shave the wool off it.

'I can't believe they're doing that after all our hard work,' exclaimed Ormsby.

'I think they're going to try and cook it,' said Arabella.

'In that case I think we had better remain at a safe distance,' warned the headmistress.

UGH!

The humans by now had managed to manhandle the huge object on to an enormous spit over the fire. About twenty small humans hung from a handle at one end of it and began to rotate it gently whilst the rest of the humans looked on with hungry eyes.

'I really do think they ought to have read the sparklebang code,' said Dr Van Der Graph.

'Look, its tail has started to sizzle,' said Oscar.

'It's only a matter of time now,' said Prunella.

All of a sudden, as the Mammoth Mammoth rotated on the spit, a beautiful shower of tiny sliver stars began to pour out of its ears.

‘Oooooooooooo!’ A ripple of approval went through the crowd of mammoths on top of the hill.

‘Ugh?!!’ exclaimed the humans in surprise.

Gradually the Mammoth Mammoth began to spin faster and faster, launching humans in all directions and the stars changed from silver to gold to pink.

'Mmmmmmmmmmmmmmm!' murmured the crowd of mammoths.

'UGH?' shouted the humans.

Suddenly, POP! POP! POP! Shimmering bunches of brightly coloured flowers shot up high into the sky and gently drizzled down to earth as the Mammoth Mammoth spun ever faster.

'Ahhhhhhhhhhh!' mused the mammoths on the mountain

'UGHHHH?!!!!' shouted the Cave Skool humans.

'I called that one *Alpine Glade*,' said Arabella. 'And finally my most potent creation . . . *Armageddon*!'

The Mammoth Mammoth was by now spinning at an unimaginably fast speed, the blur of vibrant colours gradually getting whiter and whiter and brighter and brighter, until finally . . .

. . . fiiiiizzzzzzzzzhiiissssssssssspizzzzzzle KA-

It exploded in a supernova of every single colour you could possibly imagine.

'BRAVO!' applauded the mammoths on top of the mountain. 'Well done!'

'UGHHHHHH!!!!' squealed the humans, who were running in all directions and generally doing anything they could to get as far away from the flaming, hissing, spitting Mammoth Mammoth monster as possible.

One of the human's fur hats had caught light and everyone agreed that the effect was quite remarkable.

Just then there was a HOOT HOOT HOOOOOT and over the horizon appeared a vast horde of very big furry animals.

'It's the herds!' exclaimed the mammoths on top of the mountain.

'They've come to rescue us!'

The herds charged.

'You've been scaring my kids!' shouted one angry mother.

'Nobody upsets my young 'uns!' shouted another.

UGH!

And the humans turned and ran away as fast as their legs could carry up through the forests and over the mountains, never to been seen in Mammothdom again.

Mammoths, owls, giant sloths, cave bears, foxes, rabbits and rodents were reunited with their mothers, fathers, brothers and sisters. And everyone was glad that everyone else was safe and sound.

'After that stupendous display put on by all the students of the first year, I think it's time to return to the Academy and begin the Founder's Fiesta!' announced the headmistress.

And they did.

The herds had brought vast quantities of food with them.

'We thought you might be hungry,' they said.

The tables were groaning under the weight. Cook quickly rustled up some enormous Founder's Fiesta puddings and blackberry juice. And so began one of the most memorable Founder's Fiestas ever.

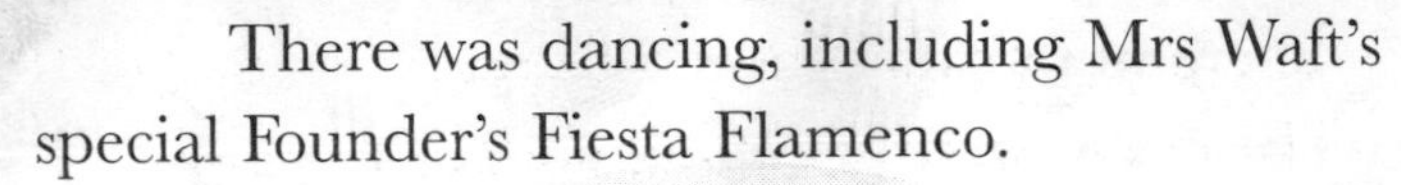

There was dancing, including Mrs Waft's special Founder's Fiesta Flamenco.

There were party games.

There was trumpeting.

There was feasting.

Everything you could ever want from a party and more!

CHAPTER 9
FINALLY

And so another Mammoth Academy term ended.

And even though the partying and the celebrating continued long into the night and way past everyone's bedtime, the stories of Arabella's magical exploding mammoth, Prunella's bravery and all the events leading up to it would be told for many many mammoth years to come.

And everybody got top marks for their project.

A+
A+
A+

Another mammoth adventure from Smarties Award winner Neal Layton

Q. What's the difference between a Woolly Mammoth and a gooseberry?

A. Woolly Mammoths don't grow on bushes

Oscar was a Woolly Mammoth, and so was Arabella. They lived a long time ago in the Ice Age...

Oscar and Fox have heard all about HUMANS – horrible hairless beings with big bashing clubs. And one day while out on a BIG ADVENTURE, they finally learn the most important lesson in Mammothdom –

HOW TO SURVIVE!

'This book gets 10/10...'
Professor Snout

'As funny as ever with quirky and delightful illustrations.'
Betty Bookmark

Oscar and Arabella and ORMSBY

OSCAR AND ARABELLA ARE THE BEST OF FRIENDS.

And then

ORMSBY

appears on the scene.

You know what they say:

'Two's company and three's a crowd!'

A terrific book about making new friends.

'... an eclectic mix of scribbles, prints and hilarious facial expressions ...'

Another tale from Smarties Award winner Neal Layton

HODDER
THE STORY OF EVERYTHING
BY NEAL LAYTON
Once upon a very long time ago
there was nothing.
No space, no time, no planets,
no people, no me, no you,
no nothing, until...

An ingenious novelty book about evolution.
It will literally BLOW YOU AWAY!